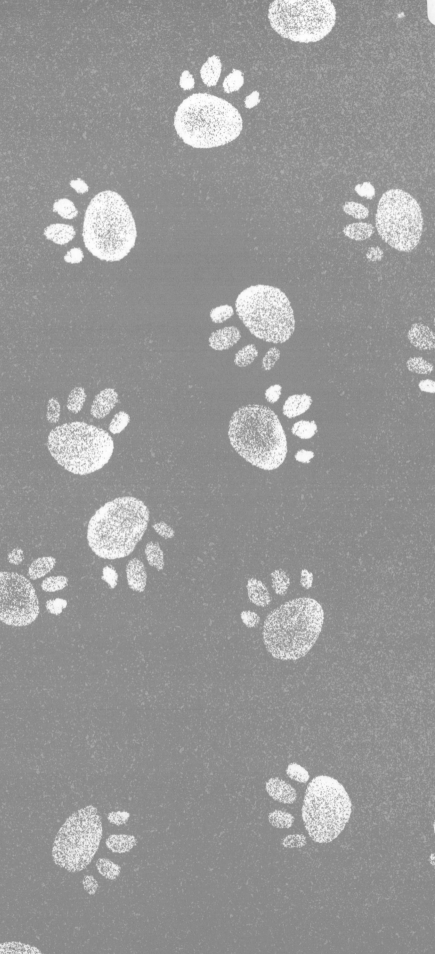

CHARLIE CHOOSES

Lou Peacock

illustrated by Nicola Slater

For Rafe. And for Charlie,
who always chooses.
Much love, LP xx

I dedicate this book to Leo . . .
actually make that to Finn.
No, Leo. No! Finn.
To Leo *and* Finn.
NS

Text by Lou Peacock
Text copyright © 2021 by Nosy Crow Ltd.
Illustrations copyright © 2021 by Nicola Slater
Nosy Crow and its logos are trademarks of Nosy Crow Ltd. Used under license.

First US edition 2021
First UK edition published by Nosy Crow Ltd. (UK) 2021

Library of Congress Catalog Card Number pending
ISBN 978-1-5362-1727-8

21 22 23 24 25 26 APS 10 9 8 7 6 5 4 3 2 1

Printed in Humen, Dongguan, China

This book was typeset in Futura.
The illustrations were created digitally.

Nosy Crow
an imprint of
Candlewick Press
99 Dover Street
Somerville, Massachusetts 02144

www.nosycrow.com
www.candlewick.com

CHARLIE CHOOSES

Lou Peacock

illustrated by Nicola Slater

An imprint of Candlewick Press

Charlie did not
like to choose.

He never knew what was best . . .

and Charlie always worried
that he might choose . . .

the wrong thing.

YUM

He could never choose between
chocolate ice cream and vanilla
ice cream, which sometimes
meant that he had . . .

no ice cream at all.

He couldn't choose between
polka-dot underwear and striped underwear,
so he often did the easiest thing . . .

and wore no underwear at all.

And bedtime was
never easy.

Light off.

Light on.

Light off.

Light on.

"I can't choose!"
said Charlie.
"It's too hard!"

So sometimes he
didn't sleep at all.

Poor Charlie knew he would never be able to choose a present for his birthday, so he looked through a book for inspiration.

The book was full of ideas . . .

a banana, a race car, a top hat, a hot dog,
an ant farm, a teddy bear, a guitar, a bucket,
a fancy dessert, a button, a pair of socks . . .

"I can't choose!"
said Charlie.

"It's too hard!"

Charlie sat down
on a park bench.

Suddenly . . .

he had an idea.

"That's it!" said Charlie.

"A dog! A dog is
the perfect present."

And off he went to the animal shelter.

The animal shelter
was full of dogs.

There were small dogs . . .

and tall dogs.

Fluffy dogs
and scruffy dogs.

White dogs
and black dogs.

Merry dogs and hairy dogs.

Floppy dogs
and
hoppy dogs.

Long dogs and strong dogs.

Old dogs and bold dogs.

And every other kind of dog.

"I can't choose,"
whispered Charlie. "It's too hard."

He started to leave . . .

but then something waggy and shaggy . . .

and mostly white, but a little bit brown . . .

scampered . . .

and jumped . . .

and dug a very big hole . . .

and ran and ran and ran . . .

right into Charlie's arms!

"Oh!" said Charlie.

"I don't have to choose!
Because this dog . . .

has chosen me."

Now Charlie has someone who helps him
choose ice cream . . .

and pick the
perfect underwear.

And, when it's bedtime,
Charlie knows exactly what to do . . .

Light off . . .
and dog on the bed.

Now all Charlie has to do is choose a name . . .